HORRiD HENRY'S
Underpants

HORRID HENRY'S
Underpants

Francesca Simon
Illustrated by Tony Ross

Orion
Children's Books

Horrid Henry's Underpants originally appeared in
Horrid Henry's Underpants first published in Great Britain in 2003
by Orion Children's Books
This edition first published in Great Britain in 2009
by Orion Children's Books
a division of the Orion Publishing Group Ltd
Orion House
5 Upper St Martin's Lane
London WC2H 9EA
An Hachette UK Company

Colour reproduction by Pixel Colour Imaging
Printed in China

www.orionbooks.co.uk
www.horridhenry.co.uk

For my nephew, Jesse Benedek Simon

Look out for . . .

Contents

Chapter 1

A late birthday present! Whoopee!
Just when you thought you'd got all
your loot, more treasure arrives.
Horrid Henry shook the small
thin package.

It was light. Very light. Maybe it was
– oh, please let it be . . .

MONEY! Of course it was money.
What else could it be?

There was so much stuff he needed:

a Mutant Max lunchbox,

a Rapper Zapper Blaster,

and, of course,
the new Terminator Gladiator game
he kept seeing advertised on TV.

Mum and Dad were so mean and
horrible, they wouldn't buy it for
him. But he could buy whatever he
liked with his own money. So there.
Ha ha ha ha ha.

Wouldn't Ralph be green with envy when he swaggered into school with a Mutant Max lunchbox? And no way would he even let Peter touch his Rapper Zapper Blaster.

So how much money had he been sent? Maybe enough for him to buy everything! Horrid Henry tore off the wrapping paper.

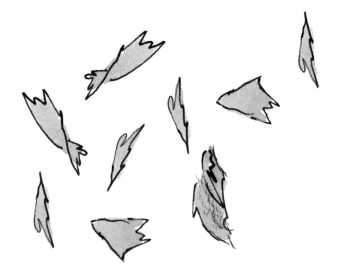

Aaaaarrrggghhhh!

Great-Aunt Greta had done it again.

Great-Aunt Greta thought he was a girl. Great-Aunt Greta had been told ten billion times that his name was Henry, not Henrietta, and that he wasn't four years old.

But every year Peter would get £10,
or a football, or a computer game,
and Henry would get a Walkie-
Talkie-Teasy-Weasy-Burpy-Slurpy
Doll. Or a Princess Pamper Parlour.
Or Baby Poopie Pants.

And now this.

Horrid Henry picked up the birthday card. Maybe there was money inside. He opened it.

Dear Henny,

You must be such a big girl now, so I know you'd love a pair of big girl pants. I'll bet pink is your favourite colour.

Love,

Great-Aunt Greta

Horrid Henry stared in horror at the
frilly pink lacy knickers, decorated
with glittery hearts and bows.

This was the worst present
he had ever received.

Worse than socks.

Worse than handkerchiefs.

Even worse
than a book.

Bleccch! Ick! Yuck!

Horrid Henry chucked the hideous
underpants in the bin where they
belonged.

Ding dong.

Oh no!

Rude Ralph was here to play. If he
saw those knickers Henry would
never hear the end of it. His name
would be mud for ever.

Clump clump clump.

Ralph was stomping up the stairs to his bedroom.

Henry snatched the terrible pants
from the bin and looked around his
room wildly for a hiding place.

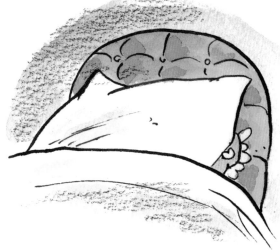

Under the pillow? What if they had
a pillow fight?

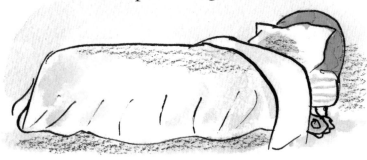

Under the bed? What if they played
hide and seek?

Quickly Henry stuffed them in the back of his pants drawer. I'll get rid of them the moment Ralph leaves, he thought.

Chapter 2

"Mercy, Your Majesty, mercy!"

King Henry the Horrible looked down at his snivelling brother. "Off with his head!" he ordered.

"Henry! Henry! Henry!" cheered his grateful subjects.

"HENRY!"

King Henry the Horrible woke up.
His Medusa mother was looming
above him.

"You've overslept!" shrieked Mum.
"School starts in five minutes!
Get dressed! Quick! Quick!"
She pulled the duvet off Henry.
"Wha-wha?" mumbled Henry.

Dad raced into the room.
"Hurry!" shouted Dad. "We're late!"
He yanked Henry out of bed.

Henry stumbled around his dark
bedroom. Half-asleep, he reached
inside his underwear drawer, grabbed
a pair, then picked up some clothes
off the floor and flung everything on.
Then he, Dad, and Peter ran all the
way to school.

"Margaret! Stop pulling Susan's hair!"

"Ralph! Sit down!"

"Linda! Sit up!"

"Henry! Pay attention!" barked Miss Battle-Axe. "I am about to explain long division. I will only explain it once. You take a great big number, like 374, and then divide it—"

Horrid Henry was not paying
attention. He was tired. He was
crabby. And for some reason his
pants were itchy. These pants feel
horrible, he thought. And so tight.
What's wrong with them?

Horrid Henry sneaked a peek.
And then Horrid Henry saw what
pants he had on.

Not his Driller Cannibal pants.

Not his Marvin the Maniac ones either.

Not even his old Gross-Out ones,
with the holes and the droopy elastic.

He, Horrid Henry, was wearing frilly
pink lacy girls' pants covered in
glittery hearts and bows.

He'd completely forgotten he'd
stuffed them into his pants drawer last
month so Ralph wouldn't see them.
And now, oh horror of horrors,
he was wearing them.

Maybe it's a **nightmare**, thought
Horrid Henry hopefully.
He pinched his arm. Ouch! Then,
just to be sure, he pinched William.

"Waaaaah!" wailed Weepy William.

"Stop weeping, William!" said Miss Battle-Axe. "Now, what number do I need—"

It was not a **nightmare**. He was still in school, still wearing pink pants.

Chapter 3

What to do, what to do?

Don't panic,

thought Horrid Henry. He took a deep breath. Don't panic.

After all, no one will know. His trousers weren't see-through or anything.

WAIT.

What trousers was he wearing? Were there any holes in them? Quickly Horrid Henry twisted round to check his bottom.

Phew. There were no holes. What luck he hadn't put on his old jeans with the big rip, but a new pair. He was safe.

"Henry! What's the answer?" said Miss Battle-Axe.

"Pants," said Horrid Henry before he could stop himself.

The class burst out laughing.

"Pants!" screeched Rude Ralph.

"Pants!" screeched Dizzy Dave.

"Henry. Stand up," ordered
Miss Battle-Axe.
Henry stood. His heart was
pounding.

Slip!
Slip!
Slip!
Slip!
Slip!
Aaaarrrghhh!

The lacy ruffle of his pink pants
was showing!
His new trousers were too big.

Mum always bought him clothes that were way too big so he'd grow into them. These were the falling-down ones he'd tried on yesterday. Henry gripped his trousers tight and yanked them up.

"What did you say?" said Miss Battle-
Axe slowly.

"Ants,"

said Horrid
Henry.

"Ants?"

said Miss Battle-Axe.

"Yeah," said Henry quickly. "I was
just thinking about how many ants
you could divide by – by that
number you said," he added.

Miss Battle-Axe glared at him.
"I've got my eye on you, Henry,"
she snapped. "Now sit down
and pay attention."

Henry sat. All he had to do was tuck in his T-shirt. That would keep his trousers up. He'd look stupid but for once Henry didn't care.

Just so long as no one ever knew about his pink lacy pants.

And then Henry's blood turned to ice. What was the latest craze on the playground?

De-bagging.
Who'd started it?
Horrid Henry.
Yesterday he'd chased
Dizzy Dave and
pulled down his trousers.

The day before he'd
done the same thing
to Rude Ralph.

Just this morning he'd
de-bagged Tough Toby
on the way into class.
They'd all be trying
to de-bag him now.

I have to get another pair of pants,
thought Henry desperately.

Miss Battle-Axe passed round the maths worksheets. Quickly Horrid Henry scribbled down: 3, 7, 41, 174, without reading any questions. He didn't have time for long division. Where could he find some other pants? He could pretend to be sick and get sent home from school. But he'd already tried that twice this week.

Wait. Wait. He was brilliant. He was a genius. What about Lost and Found? Someone, some time, must have lost some pants.

Chapter 4

Ding! Ding!

Before the playtime bell had finished
ringing Horrid Henry was out of his
seat and racing down the hall,
holding tight to his trousers.

He checked carefully to make sure no one was watching, then he ducked into Lost and Found. He'd hide here until he found some pants.

The Lost and Found was stuffed with
clothes. He rummaged through the
mountains of

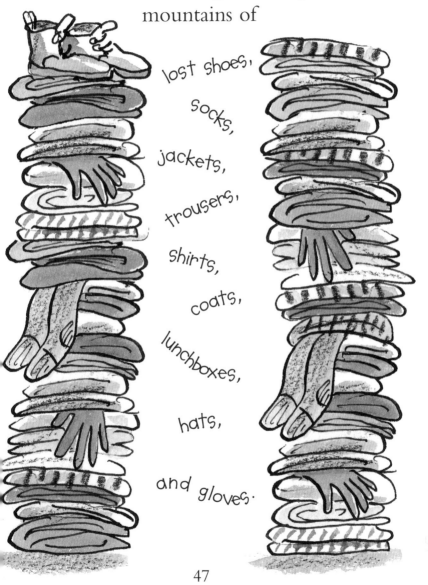

lost shoes,

socks,

jackets,

trousers,

shirts,

coats,

lunchboxes,

hats,

and gloves.

I'm amazed anyone leaves school wearing *anything*, thought Horrid Henry, tossing another sweatshirt over his shoulder.

Then – hurray! Pants. A pair of blue pants. What a wonderful sight.

Horrid Henry pulled the pants from
the pile. Oh no. They were the
teeniest, tiniest pair he'd ever seen.
Some toddler must have lost them.

Rats, thought Horrid Henry. Well, no way was he wearing his horrible pink pants a second longer. He'd just have to trade pants with someone. And Horrid Henry had the perfect someone in mind.

Chapter 5

Henry found Peter in the playground
playing tag with Tidy Ted.
"I need to talk to you in private,"
said Henry. "It's urgent."
"What about?" said Peter cautiously.

"It's top secret," said Henry. Out of
the corner of his eye he saw Dave
and Toby sneaking towards him.
Top secret! Henry never shared top
secret secrets with Peter.

"Quick!" yelped Henry. "There's no
time to lose!"
He ducked into the boys' toilet.
Peter followed.

"Peter, I'm worried about you," said
Horrid Henry. He tried to look
concerned.
"I'm fine," said Peter.

"No you're not," said Henry. "I've
heard bad things about you."
"What bad things?" said Peter
anxiously. Not − not that he had run
across the carpet in class?

"Embarrassing rumours," said Horrid Henry. "But if I don't tell you, who will? After all," he said, putting his arm around Peter's shoulder, "it's my job to look after you. Big brothers should look out for little ones."

Perfect Peter could not believe his ears.
"Oh, Henry," said Peter.
"I've always wanted a brother who looked after me."

"That's me," said Henry. "Now listen.
I've heard you wear baby pants."
"I do not," said Peter. "Look!" And
he showed Henry his Daffy and her
Dancing Daisies pants.

Horrid Henry's heart went cold.
Daffy and her Dancing Daisies!

Ugh.

Yuck.

Gross.

But even Daffy would be a million
billion times better than pink pants
with lace ruffles.

"Daffy Daisy are the most babyish pants you could wear," said Henry. "Worse than wearing a nappy. Everyone will tease you."

Peter's lip trembled. He hated being teased. "What can I do?" he asked.

Henry pretended to think. "Look.
I'll do you a big favour. I'll swap
my pants for
yours. That way
I'll get teased,
not you."

"Thank you,
Henry," said Peter.
"You're the best brother in
the world." Then he stopped.

"Wait a minute," he said suspiciously.
"Let's see your pants."
"Why?" said Henry.
"Because," said Peter, "how do
I know you've even got pants
to swap?"

Horrid Henry was outraged.
"Of course I've got pants,"
said Henry.
"Then show me," said Peter.

Horrid Henry was trapped.
"OK," he said, giving Peter
a quick flash of pink lace.

Perfect Peter stared at Henry's
underpants.
"Those are your pants?" he said.
"Sure," said Horrid Henry.
"These are big boy pants."

"But they're **pink**," said Peter.

"All big boys wear **pink**," said Henry.

"But they have *lace* on them,"
said Peter.

"All big boys' pants have *lace*,"
said Henry.

"But they have
hearts and bows,"
said Peter.

"Of course they do, they're big boy pants," said Horrid Henry. "You wouldn't know because you only wear baby pants."

Peter hesitated. "But . . . but . . . they look like – girls' pants," said Peter.

Henry snorted. "Girls' pants! Do you think *I'd* ever wear girls' pants? These are what all the cool kids are wearing. You'll be the coolest kid in the class in these."

Perfect Peter backed away.
"No I won't," said Peter.
"Yes you will," said Henry.
"I don't want to wear your smelly
pants," said Peter.
"They're not smelly," said Henry.
"They're brand new. Now give me
your pants."

"NO!" screamed Peter.

"YES!" screamed Henry.
"Give me your pants!"

"What's going on in here?" came a
voice of steel. It was the Head,
Mrs Oddbod.
"Nothing," said Henry.
"There's no hanging about the toilets
at playtime," said Mrs Oddbod.
"Out of here, both of you."

Peter ran out of the door.
Now what do I do? thought Horrid
Henry.

Henry ducked into a stall and hid the pink pants on the ledge above the third toilet.

No way was he putting those pants back on. Better Henry-no-pants than Henry-pink-pants.

Chapter 6

At lunchtime Horrid Henry dodged
Graham. He dodged Toby by the
climbing frame.

During last play Dave almost caught him by the water fountain but Henry was too quick.

Ralph chased him into class but Henry got to his seat just in time.

He'd done it!

Only forty-five minutes to go until home time. There'd be no de-bagging after school with parents around.

Henry couldn't believe it. He was
safe at last.
He stuck out his tongue at Ralph.

Miss Battle-Axe clapped her claws.
"Time to change for P.E.,"
said Miss Battle-Axe.

P.E! It couldn't be – not a P.E. day.
"And I don't care if aliens stole your
P.E. kit, Henry," said Miss Battle-Axe,
glaring at him. "No excuses."

That's what she thought. He had the
perfect excuse. Even a teacher as
mean and horrible as Miss Battle-Axe
would not force a boy to do P.E.
without pants. Horrid Henry went
up to Miss Battle-Axe and whispered
in her ear.

"Forgot your pants, eh?"
barked Miss Battle-Axe loudly.
Henry blushed scarlet. When he was
king he'd make Miss Battle-Axe walk
around town every day wearing pants
on her head.

"Well, Henry, today is your lucky
day," said Miss Battle-Axe, pulling
something pink and lacy out of her
pocket. "I found these in the boys'
toilets."

"Take them away!"

screamed Horrid Henry.

More HORRID HENRY

Colour books

Horrid Henry's Big Bad Book
Horrid Henry's Wicked Ways
Horrid Henry's Evil Enemies
Horrid Henry Rules the World
Horrid Henry's House of Horrors
Horrid Henry's Dreadful Deeds

Activity Books

Horrid Henry's Brainbusters
Horrid Henry's Headscratchers
Horrid Henry's Mindbenders
Horrid Henry's Colouring Book
Horrid Henry's Puzzle Book
Horrid Henry's Sticker Book
Horrid Henry's Mad Mazes
Horrid Henry's Wicked Wordsearches
Horrid Henry's Crazy Crosswords
Horrid Henry's Classroom Chaos
Horrid Henry's Holiday Havoc
Horrid Henry Runs Riot